# Pick
## YOUR OWN
## Quest

# Series by Connor Hoover

*Wizards of Tomorrow*
*Alien Treasure Hunters*
*Pick Your Own Quest*

# Pick Your Own Quest Books

*Pick Your Own Quest: King Tut's Adventure*
*Pick Your Own Quest: Escape From Minecraft*
*Pick Your Own Quest: Return to Minecraft*
*Pick Your Own Quest: Minecraft The End*
*Pick Your Own Quest: Trapped in A Fairy Tale*

# Pick Your Own Quest

# Trapped in a Fairy Tale

by
CONNOR HOOVER

ROOTS IN MYTH, AUSTIN, TX

Pick Your Own Quest: Trapped in a
Fairy Tale

A Root in Myth Book
Austin, Texas
For more information, write
connor@connorhoover.com

www.connorhoover.com

Paperback ISBN: 978-1-949717-09-9

For Fairy Tale Lovers Everywhere

**D**on't read this book like other books. If you read this book from front to back, nothing will make sense. But if you follow the instructions on each page, the story will come to life. Okay, the forty-two stories. Because that's how this book works.

There are forty-two different stories inside. Read the words on the page. Then, when it tells you to make a choice, you turn to the page that it tells you to turn to. One thing you have to keep in mind. You can't turn back.

If you're expecting a happily ever after every time, put this book down now. Your chances are pretty slim. Sure, there is a handful of happy endings, but with over forty possible ways to finish the story, they can't all end with puppies and chocolate.

*If you dare, turn the page.*

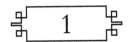

You ou drive twelve hours to your grandmother's house. When you finally pull into the driveway, you can't wait to run and play in the backyard. There are so many fun things to do at Granny's house. You can feed the geese. You can run up and down the hill. You can fish off the dock. Except the second you step out of the car, a giant raindrop falls on your head. Then another. And another. Pretty soon it's pouring. Thunder rumbles in the sky and lighting strikes down so close your hairs stand on end. You rush inside. You can play outside tomorrow.

"Let's read a book," Granny says. She's holding the biggest book you've ever seen in your life. If she opens that thing, you know you're going to spend your entire vacation reading. You almost suggest playing a video

game instead, but she looks so hopeful, and you don't want to crush her dreams. Also, she has a giant mug of hot chocolate that she sets on a table nearby. It's so hot that it's still letting off steam.

You sit down and she dumps the book on your lap. It must weigh fifty pounds.

"Oh, I almost forgot about something," Granny says, patting you on the head. "Wait right here."

Granny disappears through a door, pulling it closed behind her. You always thought it was a closet, but maybe it's a bathroom you never knew about. She could have remodeled. You wait for her to get back. But she takes forever. You want a sip of hot chocolate, but it's still too hot to drink.

"Granny?" you finally say.

No answer.

You knock on the closet door. Still nothing. You want to check on her, but what if it is a bathroom? The last thing you want to see is your granny going potty. Still, what if she's in trouble?

You slowly turn the knob and open the door.

It is a closet, just like you thought. But there's no sign of your Granny anywhere. You step inside because maybe she's in the far back. It's really dark and you can't see anything.

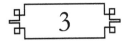

"Granny?"

"In here," she says.

Whew! You move toward the back of the closet, but you still don't see her. You turn back, but the door you just came through is gone! Instead, back the way you came is a forest with trees and birds and everything! You must be dreaming.

Ahead, you're sure you see something. It looks like . . . No, that's not possible. You rub your eyes. You were right. Ahead of you is a castle! A real life castle with flags and turrets. Maybe Granny went to the castle. Or maybe she's in the forest.

---

*If you head for the forest, turn to page 5.*

*If you check out the castle, turn to page 6.*

No way are you going into some random castle. It might be ruled by an evil king. Or a mean queen. It's not a smart thing to do, and Granny would know that. Instead you turn and head for the forest.

There's a nice lit-up path leading into it, and you start off down the path. It almost looks like people come this way often. This is a great sign. Granny will surely be down this way. But pretty soon the path gets really ragged and the trees get thicker and it gets dark.

That's okay. You aren't scared of the dark. You take another step, and out of the silence a wolf starts howling. It's immediately joined by another. Then another. Uh oh. If this pack of wolves finds you, they're going to eat you for supper. You need shelter.

You look around for a little bit to see if there happens to be some shelter nearby, but you don't find any. It's getting darker every second. You could make your own shelter, or you could keep looking.

*If you make your own shelter, turn to page 10.*

*If you keep looking for shelter, turn to page 12.*

The castle means people. That's where Granny is bound to be. You start across a grassy meadow toward the castle. You don't see any sign of Granny, but what if she's trapped in here? You have to find her. Maybe someone has seen her.

You look around as you walk but don't see anyone. Wait! Someone is coming right toward you. Maybe they've seen your granny. As the person gets closer, you see that it's an old lady. Not your granny, but maybe they're friends.

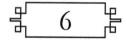

"Excuse me, have you seen a little old lady?" you ask the woman. She's holding an apple in one hand and a stick in the other.

She opens her mouth to answer, and you realize that she has no teeth. Guess she won't be eating the apple.

"I haven't seen anyone," the old lady says. "But do you want an apple?" She holds it out to you. Her fingernails are black which is really gross.

You step back. "No thanks. I'm going to look in the castle for my granny."

"Oh, the castle," the old woman says. "They're expecting you."

That's creepy and weird. She starts walking away. You think about asking her what she meant, but you don't really want to talk to her anymore. She kind of freaks you out. Still, what did she mean? They're expecting you? Maybe you should sneak in the castle instead.

*If you sneak around back to find a secret way into the castle, turn to page 8.*

*If you go through the open drawbridge and front gate of the castle, turn to page 9.*

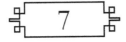

N o way are you going in the front door of the castle after what the old lady said. It could be a trap. You sneak around the back. The castle is way bigger than you thought, and it takes you a long time. Also, you try to hide behind things, because if someone is watching you, you don't want to be seen.

Finally you reach the back of the castle. You look everywhere for some kind of door, but you can't find one. There is a tower, though, and a bright red light comes from it. Red is Granny's favorite color. Maybe she's trapped in the tower and she's trying to signal you to let you know. You should look for a ladder and climb up to see what's going on up there.

You glance off to the right and spot a trail of breadcrumbs leading away from the tower and castle. Wait! Bread is Granny's favorite food. Maybe she left you the trail of breadcrumbs to follow.

*If you look for a ladder to get into the tower, turn to page 14.*

*If you follow the trail of breadcrumbs, turn to page 20.*

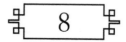

That's actually great that the people in the castle are expecting you. It could be Granny!

You cross the drawbridge. The metal grate at the castle entrance is open, and you walk through. As soon as you are under it, it slams closed. Oops. Hope there's another way out. It looks pretty heavy, and you aren't sure you can lift it. But first, you need to look for Granny.

"Hello," you call into the castle.

No one answers you. If there are people in here waiting for you, they're being kind of quiet. You walk inside. Paintings and tapestries cover the walls, and you've never seen so many fancy things in all your life.

You wander around and finally see a dining room! It has a huge table that stretches from one end to the next, and it is covered with food. A sign in the middle of the table says ALL YOU CAN EAT BUFFET.

Sweet! You are really hungry, and you run over and start stuffing your face with all the amazing food.

*Turn to page 22.*

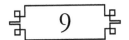

You can't waste any more time looking for shelter. You are going to have to make your own. You aren't some master house builder, but you'll have to do your best.

You look around and notice a pile of straw, and as fast as you can, you make a small house out of it. You run inside just as the wolves howl again. Phew. That was close. Now it's time to get some sleep. But you've hardly closed your eyes when the howls of the wolves get closer. And closer. And the next thing you know the straw flies away from you like a giant wind came along

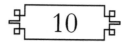

and blew it down. In front of you is the biggest wolf you've ever seen (not that you've seen that many). You run.

Once you're far enough away from the wolf, you find a pile of sticks. These are much better to build a shelter with. But the same thing happens. No sooner do you finish your shelter and crawl inside, the same wolf comes along and blows it down. It's almost like this is some kind of game to him.

By now it's really dark. If you don't get somewhere safe, that wolf is going to eat you. Luckily you find a pile of bricks. There is no way a wolf will be able to blow these down. You can build your shelter out of these. Except the wolf howls, and it's really close. Maybe you should run away and look for shelter instead because it will take a really long time to build a house out of bricks.

---

*If you build a house out of bricks, turn to page 48.*

*If you run away and look for shelter, turn to page 16.*

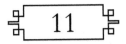

There is no time to make your own shelter. Those wolves will be here before you know it. The only way to stay alive is to find a place to hide. There has to be somewhere.

It is getting darker every second. You run as fast as you can, staying alert and looking. Finally your search pays off. Ahead of you is a cave hidden behind a tree. Maybe the wolves don't know about it. You're about to dash toward the cave when you look back one time.

You see smoke, curling out of the top of a chimney. How had you missed that earlier?

*If you go into the cave, turn to page 24.*

*If you run toward the smoke and chimney, turn to page 18.*

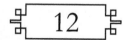

This Mama and Papa Bear seem to be so happy to have found you. You don't want to make them sad. You also don't want them to eat you. So you play along and pretend to be Baby Bear.

Mama and Papa Bear make you porridge three times a day. After a couple days, they tell you that they signed you up for bear preschool. At school, all the other bears pretend you are a bear, too. They teach you all sorts of useful bear skills, like digging in trash cans, scaring humans, and scratching your back on trees. These bear things are actually kind of fun, and you're pretty good at them.

As fun as being a bear is, you still want to get back to your real home. You can't pretend to be a bear the rest of your life. But if you leave Mama and Papa Bear, it is going to make them very sad.

*If you leave Mama and Papa Bear, turn to page 64.*

*If you stay a little bit longer, turn to page 84.*

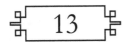

You look everywhere for a ladder but don't see one. Wait, there is a cellar door. Maybe it leads into the castle. You didn't see it before. You head down into the cellar. There's all sorts of weird stuff stashed everywhere, like old suits of armor and giant swords as tall as you. There are also shelves lined with potions and powders. You try not to touch anything because the last thing you need is some spell being cast on you. There's no way into the castle from down here, but there is a ladder. You drag the ladder out and lean it against the tower. It barely reaches the top.

You start climbing. You have to lean really far to wrap your fingers around the windowsill, but you make it. You pull yourself inside. But your heel catches on the ladder, and it falls away from the tower, all the way to the ground. Guess you won't be using the ladder to get out of here.

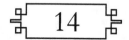
14

You look around the tower. The red light is coming from a red lantern in the center of the room. Granny is not there, but something is written on a chalkboard. It says, "Granny was here." That's a really good sign. Except now you're stuck in the tower.

The tower has only the one window, no steps, and no door. You sink down onto a chair and try to figure a way out of here. That's when a golden candlestick bursts to life and starts talking to you.

"Ya want outta here?" it says.

This is a pretty dumb question. Does it think you want to stay here forever?

"Well, yeah, I want out of here, but I'm trapped," you say.

"I can show ya the way out," the candlestick says. "But ya have to make a bargain."

Maybe Granny made the same bargain and that's how she got out of here. But you don't know anything about this candlestick. It could be trying to trick you.

---

*If you make the bargain, turn to page 38.*

*If you don't make the bargain, turn to page 26.*

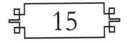

15

You run and run, looking everywhere for shelter. The wolf is right behind you and getting closer with every second. You need to do something.

In the dark you run into a tree, except it has really smooth bark, not like any tree you've ever seen. Not that you care what kind of tree it is. You start climbing. You can't remember if wolves can climb. You really hope not.

The tree twists and turns, and once it reaches above all the other trees, the sun comes out and you realize that it's actually a giant beanstalk. You're a little scared of being up so high, but you're more scared of wolves, so you keep climbing. It reaches through the clouds

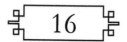

until finally it ends at a land hidden up in the sky. Maybe there's a way back to your world from this sky land.

You start walking and pretty soon you see a castle. You didn't go into the other castle, but maybe this one is okay. What other option do you have?

You creep inside, because if there is an angry king around, you don't want to disturb him. But you don't see a king or anyone for that matter. All you see is a golden goose that is as big as you are. You surprise it because it lets out a honk and then lays an egg. A shiny golden egg that is as big as your head.

You would really like that egg.

---

*If you take the egg, turn to page 28.*

*If you don't take the egg because that would be stealing, turn to page 40.*

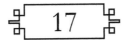

oing into a cave would be stupid. You might run away from wolves only to be eaten by lions or tigers or bears. You have no idea about anything in this land where you are. You need to be careful. You run toward the smoke and the chimney.

You are sure at any second that the wolves will catch you, but you make it to the smoke. In a neat little clearing is a small two-story cottage. You don't stop to think. You run inside.

You call out, but nobody seems to be home. But there are three nice bowls of porridge sitting on the kitchen counter. Your stomach grumbles, and you realize that you are starving.

You start with the biggest bowl, eat the entire thing, then the medium bowl, and finally the smallest bowl. You're still a little hungry, but you did just eat three bowls of porridge, and you don't want to make whoever lives here mad.

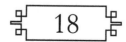

You go into the living room to sit down, but you break the first chair you sit in. Then you break the next chair. And the next. Who made these chairs anyway? They need to get some better craftspeople. Finally the food catches up with you, and you get really tired. You climb into the first bed you see and fall fast asleep.

You wake up with your heart pounding. Standing over you are two giant bears. They are going to eat you! But the one with the pink bow in her hair reaches down and pats you on the head.

"There you are, Baby Bear," she says. "We've been looking everywhere for you."

You don't look like a baby and you don't look like a bear. You're about to tell them this, but then you remember that it's not a good idea to make a bear mad. Making two bears mad is even worse. Maybe you should play along.

---

*If you tell them you have no idea who Baby Bear is, but that it definitely isn't you, turn to page 30.*

*If you play along and pretend to be Baby Bear, turn to page 13.*

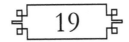

19

Granny totally left you a trail of breadcrumbs. She probably didn't want you to be bored on your vacation, and this is all a fun game to her.

You set out following the trail of breadcrumbs. But the trail is really long, and you start getting hungry. You reach down and grab some of the crumbs and eat them. They're super sweet, almost like they're cookie crumbs, not breadcrumbs. That's okay. Granny loves cookies. And so do you. You eat a lot more of the crumbs.

You walk a bit more and hear someone crying. Around the corner, sitting against a tree, is a girl about your same age.

"Who are you, and why are you crying?" you ask.

She wipes her eyes. "My name is Gretel, and an evil witch kidnapped my brother. I think she's going to do something horrible to him. Will you help me save him?"

Help save him? You don't even know him. And evil witches are nothing to mess around with. Still, if some evil witch captured you, you would want someone to help free you. But you need to find Granny. She could be in trouble.

"Please?" Gretel says.

---

*If you help Gretel find her brother, turn to page 32.*

*If you tell Gretel that you can't help her, turn to page 42.*

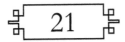

You wake up on a sofa. You hadn't even known that you'd fallen asleep. Maybe it was from all the food that you ate.

From off to your left, you hear a lady talking. But she doesn't seem to be talking to you.

"Mirror, Mirror, on the wall . . . ," she says.

You remember some story where you heard about someone saying this, but you can't remember all the details. All those fairy tale stories kind of blend together. You barely open one eye and look.

A woman is standing in front of a mirror, talking to it. She might not even know you're here. You think a little harder, and if you remember right, the woman in the story who talked to the mirror was evil. But this woman doesn't look evil. She actually looks really nice. And pretty.

You try to decide if you should say something to her or wait for her to leave and then look around on your own. After all, just because she looks nice doesn't mean she is nice.

---

*If you say hello to the woman, turn to page 34.*

*If you wait for the woman to leave, turn to page 44.*

The cave might be dark, but it's right here in front of you. If you tried to run for the chimney, the wolf could eat you. You run for the cave . . . and slam right into something blocking the way!

You fall to the ground, a little dazed. You have to do something though, so you climb a nearby tree. You manage to stay in the tree all night though you don't get much sleep. But at least the wolf doesn't eat you.

The next day you hear someone whistling. You stay really quiet, and a man approaches the cave. He's wearing brightly colored clothes, lots of fancy gold jewelry, and a sword. The sword looks really sharp. He says some funny words, and the rock in front of the cave slides open! Then he goes inside. The rock closes behind him.

Wow! You think the words he said were "Open Sesame" or something like that. Maybe you should go into the cave also.

*If you go into the cave, turn to page 36.*

*If you don't go into the cave, turn to page 46.*

The mermaid seems really nice and you want to help her. You take the shell thing, put it over your mouth, and jump into the water. You try to hold out on breathing for as long as you can, but then you have to. The shell thing works! You can breathe underwater.

The mermaid swims you to the lair of an evil sea witch. You two hide behind a rock, and even though the mermaid can't speak, she manages to get across the message that the necklace the evil sea witch is wearing actually has the mermaid's voice trapped inside. She wants you to get it back for her. You want to help the mermaid, so you come up with a plan. You could try to sneak up there and steal the necklace, or you could talk to the sea witch and hope she'll give it to you. Maybe you can trick her or something.

*If you try to steal the necklace from the sea witch, turn to page 77.*

*If you talk to the sea witch, turn to page 140.*

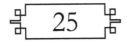

No way are you making a bargain with this talking candlestick. It's totally trying to trick you into something.

"No thanks," you say. "I have my own plan."

"Whatever," the candlestick says, and then the flame goes out and it never talks again.

Now you need a plan. You look around and see some super-hair-growing vitamins. You can make a rope with your hair. You take two each day, and your hair grows . . . an inch. This is going to take forever.

While you're looking out the window one day, a girl walks by.

"Hey! I'm trapped!" you call down to her.

"I don't believe you," she says, and she starts to walk away.

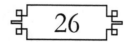

"Please! Put the ladder against the tower," you say. "I'll do anything to get out of here."

"Anything?" she says.

You nod and she leans the ladder against the tower. You are out the window and down the ladder without ever looking back. That tower was starting to smell really bad.

"Thanks," you say, and you smile because she's kind of cute.

She doesn't smile back. She says, "My name is Ella, and I do expect something in return. Will you help me do away with my evil stepmother as a return favor?"

You're here to find your granny, not do away with some old hag. But Ella did help you out of the tower.

*If you help her, turn to page 72.*

*If you don't help her, turn to page 50.*

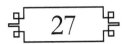

Of course you take the egg! When will you ever have a chance like this again? When you bring this thing back and show your friends, they are never going to believe it. It's kind of heavy, and there is no way it will fit in your pocket, so you find a burlap sack and throw the egg inside. Then you look for a way to get out of this place.

You're wandering around the castle looking in every room when the ground begins to shake. It's like footsteps, except giant footsteps. That's it! A giant must live in this place. Sure enough you round the corner and see a giant walking your way. You turn and run back the way you came.

"In here," someone says and yanks you into a nearby room. It's a girl wearing an apron, like she's a cook.

"Thanks for saving me," you say. "Who are you?"

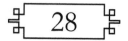

She tosses her hair back. "My name is Ella, and I didn't save you. The giant will still be able to smell you unless you hide in the oven." She points to the oven on the other side of the kitchen.

Hiding in an oven does not sound like a good idea. Your mom told you to never get in the oven, but even if she hadn't, everyone knows that. But still, you don't want this giant to sniff you out and eat you for lunch.

*If you hide in the oven, turn to page 74.*

*If you look for another hiding place, turn to page 52.*

You aren't going to pretend to be some baby bear!

"I have no idea who this Baby Bear is, but it is definitely not me," you say, sitting up in bed. "I'm a human."

The bears smile at you and pat you on the head some more, and then they lead you downstairs and offer you more porridge. You don't want more porridge. You want to get out of here before they realize their mistake. They go to the living room to sit in their (broken) chairs, and you run out the door.

It's daytime now, and the wolves are nowhere to be found. You walk toward the sound of rushing water, and there sitting by a little rock is a bear. A baby bear.

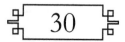

"Are you Baby Bear?" you ask the little guy. He's really cute, and he rolls over onto his back like he wants to play with you. But he doesn't seem to speak human like his parents. Still, he must be Baby Bear, and he's probably lost.

---

*If you take Baby Bear back to his parents, turn to page 54.*

*If you leave Baby Bear and keep looking for a way to get home, turn to page 76.*

Of course you have to help Gretel save her brother. You will find this evil witch and face her. It's the right thing to do.

Gretel leads you through the woods, still following the trail of cookie crumbs. Pretty soon you come to a clearing. A cute little cottage is in the center of the clearing. It's brown and decorated with . . . gumdrops! The entire cottage actually looks like a life-sized gingerbread house. You don't need cookie crumbs. You could just eat part of this house. You break off a piece of the fence and crunch on it. It tastes like peppermint.

"She has him inside," Gretel says. "But I'm scared of her. Will you go in and save him?"

You wipe your mouth because it feels like you have powdered sugar all over it. "Sure," you say. You walk

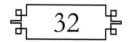

across the yard and push on the door. It's already hanging open, and it swings all the way open easily.

"Hello," you say.

Nobody answers. You dare to step inside. You look everywhere, but you don't find anyone. Gretel must have been wrong. You grab a cookie and bite into it then turn to head back outside to tell her.

Gretel is standing right by the front door.

"Your brother's not in here," you say.

"I know," Gretel says, and then she lunges for you and tries to wrap her fingers around your throat. Maybe she's the witch!

You don't want anything to do with witches. What you want to do is run away. But you also feel like it's your responsibility to fight her so she doesn't trap any more innocent kids.

---

*If you run from Gretel, turn to page 56.*

*If you fight Gretel, turn to page 78.*

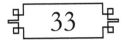

It can't hurt to say hello to the woman. After all, you could have been snoring and she might already know you are here.

"Hi," you say.

She whips around to face you. "Oh, I didn't know you were awake. You ate so much food, I thought you would sleep for one hundred years."

Just thinking about the food makes you hungry again.

The woman seems really nice, and you tell her about how you are looking for your granny. She offers to let you stay here at the castle in hopes that Granny will come here. This sounds great to you. After all, the food is amazing.

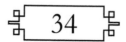

"But," she says. "I would need you to do some work around here."

You aren't afraid of a little hard work, so you happily agree.

Your job ends up being mostly cleaning, and it gets a little boring. One day you're dusting the room with the mirror when it starts talking to you. It tells you that you can step through into another world.

Maybe it means the real world where you came from! But what if it's not? You hear the woman coming, and you don't want to lose this chance, so you step through the mirror.

---

*Turn to page 58.*

You may never have another chance to say magical words and get into a secret cave. You need to do this. You say the words, and the giant rock slides open, revealing the inside of the cave.

There aren't any voices that you hear, and you don't see anyone, so you tiptoe inside. The rock slides closed behind you.

All over the cave is treasure. Bright colorful gems and shiny gold and silver and fancy crowns and swords and all sorts of stuff. You've never seen anything like it in your life. Along the wall are shelves and shelves of all your favorite foods. You grab some licorice and start eating because you are starving. Food has never tasted so good. Finally you can't eat another bite.

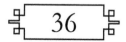

All that food made you sleepy, so you look for somewhere to take a nap. There are pillows and cushions in a corner. You tuck yourself under a fluffy cushion so no one will see you, and you fall fast asleep.

You wake to the sound of voices. People are in the cave talking. They don't seem to know you're here. They're talking about stealing more treasure.

---

*If you keep quiet and wait for them to leave, then make your escape, turn to page 80.*

*If you announce your presence and ask if you can join them, turn to page 59.*

"I accept your bargain," you tell the candlestick.

It laughs and smiles. You immediately regret your decision, but there's no changing it now.

"Follow me," it says, and it leads you to a huge painting on the wall of the tower. The painting looks like the inside of a fancy castle, complete with ornate furniture and suits of armor. "All ya have to do is step through the painting," the candlestick says.

What? It's that easy? You could have figured that out yourself.

You drag a chair over to the painting and step through. You're now inside the castle! It worked just like magic.

"I told ya I could get ya outta there," the candlestick says.

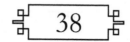

You hadn't realized it had followed you through. Whatever. Maybe it will come in handy. There's gold and crystal everywhere, and when you look down, you notice you're dressed in really fancy clothes. You walk to a mirror so you can admire yourself, but it's not your reflection you see. It's a hideous, ugly monster!

"I'm a monster!" you cry.

"Well, that was the bargain," the candlestick says.

"What am I supposed to do?"

The candlestick says, "Ya have two choices. Ya can stay here and wait for a kiss from your true love, or ya can venture out into the world and try to find your true love out there." Then the flame of the candle goes out, and it never speaks again.

*If you stay in the castle, turn to page 82.*

*If you venture out into the world, turn to page 60.*

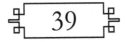

No way are you taking the egg. That would totally be stealing, and nothing good ever happens from stealing. You've read enough books and seen enough movies to know that. You leave the goose and the egg and head to the next room.

Sitting in the next room is a giant! A really big giant (like a giant giant!). He's scary and mean looking. You need to get away from him.

He sniffs the air. "I can't see you, but I can smell you," he says.

It's good that he can't see you. You start running, but maybe he can smell really well because he slams something down over your head. It's a giant birdcage, and you are now his bird.

"Sing for me, pretty bird," the giant says.

Is he crazy? You can't sing. Except he keeps asking, so finally you sing a song your granny used to sing to you.

The giant covers his ears. "That's horrible!"

You get an idea. "Well, if you would open the door to this cage, I'd be able to sing a lot better. I feel too stifled in here."

The giant seems to think about this, then he reaches out and opens the door.

Immediately you take off running. You can't sing for a giant for the rest of your life. But you aren't even to the exit when the giant starts crying.

"Please don't leave me," he cries. "I'm so sad and lonely."

You feel really bad. Maybe you should sing one more song for him before you go.

---

*If you sing one more song for the giant, turn to page 62.*

*Sad or not, you are getting out of here. Turn to page 83.*

Gretel seems just a little too shifty and you're sure she's up to no good.

"I can't help you," you say. "But I'll see if I can find someone to help you."

"Please," she says again. "You can have this candy."

You almost reconsider. Except she doesn't blink, like she's trying to hold her sad face in place. You don't trust her.

"I'll be back," you say, and you take the candy from her and run away.

You wander for a couple hours and you find a town. In town, you go into a shop that sells candy and tell someone about Gretel.

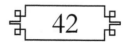

"You're very lucky you didn't trust her," the candy maker says. He takes the candy she gave you and burns it. Then he tells you that Gretel is actually a witch who traps unsuspecting travelers like you.

You ask if there is anywhere you could stay in town. You're hoping he lets you stay here because you do like candy.

"I don't need any help, but check the shoe store. I think they're hiring," he says.

You go to the shoe store, and sure enough the shoemaker offers you a job. You don't actually want a job making shoes. But you need money and a place to stay while you look for Granny.

---

*If you take the job, turn to page 86.*

*If you don't take the job, turn to page 66.*

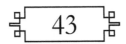

43

You're not going to just start talking to the woman. After all, who talks to mirrors? It's just weird.

The woman talks to the mirror for at least an hour. You really have to use the bathroom. Finally, when you think you can't wait any longer, she leaves the room. You jump up from the sofa and look for a bathroom. A castle this size should have at least twenty, but you can't find a single one. The gate is still locked, but there's an open window and you jump through.

You land in water. It's the moat. Finally you use the bathroom.

When you're done, you climb from the water and shake off as much water as you possible can. Now to figure out what to do. Off to the right are the woods

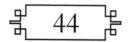

and off to the left are some mountains. The woods look scary, so you head for the mountains. Pretty soon you hear singing, and when you turn a corner, there are seven dwarves coming out of a tunnel in the mountainside.

"Lucky day!" one of them says. "We were just looking for someone to help. We found a new vein of gold, and we can't do everything. Do you want a job?"

Do you? Gold sounds pretty good, but you aren't sure about mining. Still the dwarves seem pretty nice, and most of them are smiling. There is one that looks like he frowns all the time. Maybe he just has to use the bathroom.

---

*If you take the job, turn to page 68.*

*If you tell them no thanks, turn to page 88.*

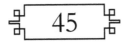

Going into a magic cave doesn't sound like a good idea. And it certainly isn't the way back to Granny and your own world. Instead you leave the cave far behind.

You travel across the land until you come to a river. It's freezing and you manage to build a small fire to keep yourself warm. As you're warming your hands, something pops up out of the water.

It's a girl. No, it's a fish. No, it's a mermaid!

She opens her mouth like she wants to talk, but no sound comes out. She motions at you then the water, like she wants you to come into the water.

You shake your head. You can't get in freezing water, and you certainly can't breathe underwater. But the

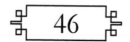

mermaid holds up a shell and puts it over her mouth and breathes. Maybe it is some kind of underwater breathing device. Then she puts her hands together, as if to say, "Please." Maybe she's in trouble and needs your help.

---

*If you help the mermaid and go into the water, turn to page 25.*

*If you don't help her because there is no way a shell can make you breathe underwater, turn to page 70.*

You looked for shelter before and didn't find any. There's no reason to think you'll find some now. Instead you start building, and you make a really nice house out of bricks in almost no time at all. If you're still alive in the morning, you can work on making it a little sturdier.

Sure enough the wolf shows up. He tries to blow your house down. You hear it howling outside like the wind. But the bricks hold.

You start getting a little hungry, and you think about how tasty wolf soup would be, so you come up with a plan.

"Bet you couldn't fit through my chimney," you call out to the wolf.

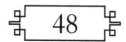

He growls and immediately climbs up your house and jumps down the chimney. He completely fits. He also fits nicely in your soup pot that you have over the fire, and once he's nicely inside, you put the lid on and make wolf soup. It's a little tough, but you can work on the recipe.

A traveler comes by the next day, and you offer her some soup. She says it's the best soup she's ever had, and she goes to the nearest town and tells everyone. The day after that five people come for your soup. The day after that, there are twenty. You are going to have to expand.

You find more bricks and expand your house into a full-on restaurant, and pretty soon you are known across the world as the best soup-maker in all of Fairy Tale Land. You keep thinking that you should find a way back to your own world, but you have too many soup customers and you never find the time.

THE END

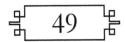

"I never signed up to do away with old ladies," you tell Ella.

"But she's really evil," Ella says.

"Not my problem," you say, and start to walk away, back toward the castle.

"You will be sorry," Ella says, and then she runs off, around the tower, and out of sight.

Whatever. You head back around the castle and over the drawbridge. You'll look for Granny inside.

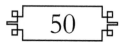

The castle is really quiet. Like not even rats are running around or anything. You tiptoe inside, and hardly breathe because you don't want anyone to know you're here, if there is anyone around.

You look in one of the rooms. There's a long dining room table with at least twenty people sitting around it. Except the food in front of them is rotten, and they are all asleep. You check a few more rooms and it's all the same thing. There are at least one hundred people in this castle, but every single one of them is snoozing.

You think you read something once about kissing a person who was sleeping in a castle and making them wake up, but you aren't really up for kissing any of these people. Still, maybe you should.

---

*If you kiss someone to wake them up, turn to page 90.*

*If you don't kiss anyone, turn to page 108.*

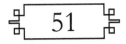

"There is no way I am hiding in some oven!" you say, and you take off running, trying to find somewhere else to hide.

Ella runs after you, and finally you guys dash outside and hide in a barrel of what you hope is only water but smells like something a lot worse. But the important thing is that the giant can't smell you.

The giant comes outside and sniffs and then looks really confused.

"He's holding me captive and making me cook for him," Ella whispers to you. "Will you help me defeat him so I can be free?"

This sounds like a pretty worthy cause so you agree. You come up with a plan to lure the giant to the edge of the land and push him over.

You jump out of the barrel of gross stuff and run, making a lot of noise. The giant hears you and starts chasing you. You're almost there. You can dash to the side and he'll keep going.

But then the giant starts yelling at you. "Don't trust the girl! She's a witch!"

Ella is a witch? Should you believe him? Or is he trying to fool you?

---

*If you believe the giant, turn to page 92.*

*If you believe Ella, turn to page 116.*

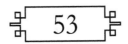

You can't leave Baby Bear here alone. After all, it might be daytime now, but when night comes again, those wolves could come along and eat him. You play with Baby Bear enough that he'll trust you, then you take his little bear paw and start leading him back to his cottage. But he doesn't want to follow. Finally you come up with a plan. It involves a trail of M&Ms that you happen to have in your pocket. Actually there seems to be a never-ending supply of them. You eat some while Baby Bear follows the trail, and pretty soon there is the cottage in front of you.

Baby Bear's parents rush out into the yard and hug Baby Bear! Your heart feels really warm just watching them, and you're happy you did the right thing. But then they turn to you.

For a brief second, you think they might eat you, but they say, "Thank you so much! Is there anything we can do to repay you?"

You tell them about how you're stuck in Fairy Tale Land and ask if they know the way out.

"We don't, but there is a leprechaun who lives not far from here who might be able to help you," Papa Bear says. "Go visit him."

---

***Turn to page 94.***

Maybe you should fight Gretel, except Gretel is an evil witch, and there is nothing good that can come from fighting an evil witch. Gretel tries to capture you and throw you into the oven, but you shove past her and run out the front door.

"Wait!" she screams at you. "Please don't leave! Please help me!"

Help her? Help her what?

You turn, and she's still there at the door. Actually, she's gnawing on the doorframe, like she's starving.

"What do you need help with?" you ask. But you're prepared to start running again once she finishes eating. You don't trust Gretel.

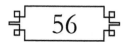

She starts crying even while she's still chewing. "It's this house," Gretel says. "It put a curse on me. I'm going to be stuck here forever, eating, if the curse isn't broken."

"Then break the curse," you say. It sounds pretty easy as far as you're concerned.

She shakes her head. "I can't. The only person who can break the curse is this old woman who lives in the nearby town. Will you go to her and ask her to break the curse?"

Is she for real? She just tried to bake you into cookies. Now she wants your help?

---

*If you help Gretel break the curse, turn to page 96.*

*If you tell her to help herself, turn to page 132.*

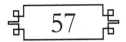

You step through the mirror and find yourself in an entirely different world. It's not the real world where you came from. You glance around and don't see Granny. You also don't see the person who was talking to you.

At first the world seems pretty normal, but then you realize that everything is opposite. Like day is night, and night is day, and when you ask someone where you are, they talk in backward sentences. It's really confusing, and you think it would take you a while to get used to it. Maybe you should step back through the mirror. Or maybe you should look around. Granny could be here somewhere. Or maybe there's a way back to your world.

---

*If you step back through the mirror, turn to page 112.*

*If you learn more about this mirror world, turn to page 98.*

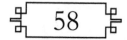

There are at least forty guys. There is no way you can stay hidden from them forever. You stand up and say, "Hello, I would love to join your band of forty thieves."

They turn and look at you, and the smiles on their faces turn to frowns.

"You know our secret," they say. "So now we need to kill you."

You promise them you would never tell anyone about them or their secret cave. At first they don't listen, but then you give them a sob story about how you are lost from your granny, and maybe they feel sorry for you. Sad stories always work.

They agree to let you join them . . . if you go on a dangerous quest. They warn you that you might get killed on the quest.

---

*If you agree to go on the quest, turn to page 114.*

*If you try to run away from them because deadly quests are not your specialty, turn to page 100.*

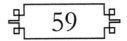

onster or not, you can't stay in this castle forever and wait for your true love to come along. That's the most ridiculous thing you've ever heard. You get a quick snack from the kitchen, put on some traveling clothes, and head out the front door of the castle.

You look everywhere for your true love. You try to explain to people what's going on, hoping they'll take pity on you, but all they do is try to stab you with pitchforks. Finally you give up and wander around looking for somewhere to live all alone. You try to find your castle, but you aren't that great with directions. You do find another castle however, and you go inside.

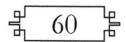

There are at least thirty other monsters in the castle, equally as hideous as you. They tell you how they made a stupid bargain with a candlestick and that's how they became monsters, and then they welcome you to their group. They tell you that for fun they go to the villages and scare people. You decide to join them.

One of the monsters tells you her name is Belle. She's kind of cute, in a monsterly sort of way, and pretty soon you think you're in love with her. You summon up the courage to kiss each other, thinking it will make you both change back into humans. It doesn't. But at least you have each other now. You live the rest of your life together as monsters.

THE END

The giant's crying is really pulling on your heartstrings, and you can't take it. You start singing.

You sing the best, sweetest, most amazing song you know, and you even add extra verses so it goes on a little bit longer. Tears slide down the giant's face as you sing, but you think they are tears of happiness. Finally you can't sing anymore. The song has to end.

"Thank you, kind songbird," the giant says. "As a reward, I will tell you how to get back to your own land."

You had not considered that. You were just trying to be nice.

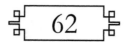

"All you have to do is get on the back of the golden goose and it will fly you back to your own land," the giant says.

The goose? "But won't you miss the goose?" you ask.

"Very much," the giant says. "But that song was worth it. Fly well, traveler."

Before he can change his mind, you leave the room and hop on the back of the goose. It immediately takes off and flies you across the giant's land, through the clouds, and to a new land.

It's your world! You see your granny's house below. The goose lands on the grass in the backyard and you climb off its back. You're sure it will fly away. But it doesn't. It lays a golden egg then jumps into the lake nearby and swims around. You're happy to be home, and you're also happy to have a new friend (especially one who lays golden eggs).

THE END

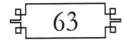

The next day when you get home from bear preschool, you tell Mama and Papa Bear that you have to leave. You play along with the whole bear thing and you tell them that you have to learn to be more independent. They cry but they say they understand. Then they warn you to be very very careful because humans do not like bears.

You aren't so worried since you aren't really a bear. You hug them goodbye, and you leave.

You wander through the woods, scratching you back on trees and looking for honeycombs. You don't see anyone the first day. But the next day you spot a man chopping down trees. Finally! It's been a long time since you've talked to another human.

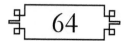

You run up to him to say hello and ask if he knows the way for you to get home. But when you talk, your voice sounds really funny.

The woodcutter raises his ax and points it right at you, and he starts talking but you can't understand a word of what he says. You look down at yourself then back at him. Wait! You really are a bear! When did that happen? How did that happen? It's impossible, and you try to explain this to the woodcutter, but he swings the ax right at you before you think to run away.

Money from a job would be nice, but you have no interest in making shoes. It actually sounds completely boring. You travel to another shop hidden in the back of town. It's run by an old woman who says that she is a spell maker. Now that sounds interesting.

"Would you like an apprentice?" you ask.

She smiles, and you notice that she has no teeth, but whatever, and she agrees. You are now the apprentice to a spell maker.

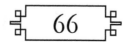

66

Spell making is very hard, but she makes sure you are careful and do everything just right. Actually she's a little too detail oriented. It kind of drives you nuts. You love when she actually leaves you alone in the shop so you can play around with the supplies on your own.

One day, she tells you that she's going to the candy store for supplies. As soon as she's out the door, you start mixing liquids together. It turns a really funny color of blue, which is cool. Then you throw in some special purple powder.

The entire thing explodes! Smoke fills the air, and you suck in and collapse into a heap on the floor. When you wake up, you are back at Granny's house sitting in the rocking chair with the huge book on your lap. The mug of hot chocolate next to you is still steaming.

Was the entire thing a dream?

THE END

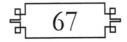

You tell the dwarves that you'd be thrilled to work with them. They all act really happy, and they lead the way back to their house. They sing the entire time, and at first the song is pretty cute, but after an hour of it, you want to plug your ears because you can't get it out of your head. It's the worst earworm in the entire world!

When you walk in the door to their house, it's the worst mess you've ever seen in your entire life.

"Start by cleaning up," one of them says. He's wearing glasses and the other dwarves call him Doc.

"Why me?" you ask.

"Because you took the job," the dwarf says.

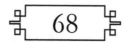

You try to tell them that you wanted a job in the mine looking for the gold, but they start laughing. Then they tell you that your job is to cook and clean for them.

No way. You make a run for the door, but they block it and won't let you go. So you cook and you clean. It would be really great if they could at least try to put their dishes away.

The next day you decide to make a run for it, but they lock you in the cellar. You try to get out, but it's no use. The next day you try again. And then you get a great idea. Actually the dwarves give you the idea, with their mines. You start digging a tunnel out of the cellar. Each day you dig a little more. Maybe in about ten years you'll finally get out of here. Until then, it's cooking and cleaning for the seven messiest dwarves in the entire universe.

THE END

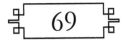

There is no way you're going to take some shell, stick it over your mouth, and jump into the water. That is a certain way to die.

"Sorry, you're going to have to find someone else to help you," you say.

Bad choice. Ten more mermaids surface and they all open their mouths at once. No sound comes out, but what they do have are very scary fangs. It's like they want to eat you! Good thing you are still on land and they are in the sea.

You turn to run, but there are the wolves! They've snuck up on you while you weren't watching. They move closer to you pushing you toward the water. This is the worst. Soon you have no choice. You jump into the water and try to swim, to evade the horrible evil mermaids. It's no use. They capture you within seconds and drag you down under the water.

At least they put the shell thing over your mouth. And hey, it does work! You can breathe!

They swim you to an evil sea witch who puts you in a cell and locks the door. Then she touches you with a different shell. You feel something leaving you, but you don't know what. When you try to open your mouth to scream, no sound comes out. Now you know how the mermaids lost their voices. Next the evil sea witch turns you into a half-fish, half-human, just like the mermaids. You are now cursed to be just like them forever.

# THE END

You help Ella because it's the right thing to do. As she leads you to her house where she says her stepmother is, she tells you how awful her stepmother has been to her. She put tar in her hair and locked Ella in an attic and never let her outside. The only nice thing the stepmother ever did was give Ella powdered sugar donuts, but they tasted awful, so Ella didn't even eat them. Ella managed to escape, but she knows her stepmother will come after her. That's why Ella wants to strike first.

By the time you reach Ella's house, you know that her stepmother is evil. And also you kind of want to spend more time with Ella, maybe even the rest of your life. An evil stepmother does not fit in to that plan.

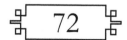

"Lock her in the attic," Ella says, and she gives you a key.

You go into the house and find the stepmother. She doesn't look any older that Ella, and she smiles and tries to charm you, but you aren't fooled.

"I'm here to check for rats in the attic," you say.

"Oh, yeah, we have a horrible rat problem," she says, and she leads you to the attic. As soon as she opens the door, you shove her inside and locked the door. She bangs on the door, but you don't let her out.

Outside you tell Ella what happened, and then you tell her of your quest to find your Granny. She vows to stay with you always and help you find Granny. You look for a year. Then another. There's no Granny and no way out of Fairy Tale Land. You vow to keep looking, but it's not so bad here. And pretty soon you forget about it altogether.

THE END

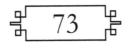

Oven or not, there is no time to look for another hiding place. The giant's footsteps are getting closer every second.

"I'll let you out once the coast is clear," Ella tells you as you climb inside. Then she closes the oven door. It has a tiny glass window that you can see through. You can also still hear the giant's footsteps.

Pretty soon the giant lumbers into the kitchen. The entire place shakes.

"Where's my meal?" the giant bellows. He's talking so loudly that it's easy to hear him.

Where will Ella tell him that you've gone? And why doesn't she need to hide?

She raises a hand and points directly at the oven, and then she smiles.

"What kind of bread do you want me to make to-day?" Ella asks the giant.

"Pumpernickel?" the giant says. "No, rye. Or maybe sourdough. He looked kind of sour."

Wait! What? They're going to bake you into bread? You try to push the oven door open, but it won't budge. You have to get out of here. This is the worst conversation you've heard in your entire life. It's also the last.

THE END

Y ou feel kind of bad leaving Baby Bear there by the river, but he's a bear. He'll get home eventually, and it's not really your problem.

You keep walking through the woods, and when you reach the edge, you see a village ahead. But an angry mob of people is coming from the village, holding torches and weapons.

"What are you doing?" you ask one of them.

The guy stops. "We're hunting bears, that's what."

You ask why, and he explains that the bears have been capturing humans and turning them into porridge. You almost throw up. You ate that porridge! But maybe the guy is wrong. And you don't want them to kill Baby Bear. Mama and Papa Bear hadn't seemed too bad either.

*If you run back into the woods to warn the bear family, turn to page 101.*

*If you tell the angry mob where the bears are, turn to page 122.*

**Y**ou wait until the sea witch isn't looking your way and then you sneak into her lair. It's filled with all sorts of cages with other creatures trapped inside. You've never seen anything like these creatures. They beg you to set them free, but you don't see any keys to help them. If you do see keys though, you'll grab them.

You wait until the sea witch falls asleep, and then you rush forward and grab the necklace. But she's not asleep after all! She grabs you and throws you into one of the cages. You've joined her collection. If only you'd looked for the keys first maybe you'd be able to get yourself out of here. Maybe the mermaid will come along and save you. Or maybe she tricked you to get you here in the first place. You'll never know.

THE END

You aren't going to run away. You fight Gretel, knocking over chairs and tables and bowls and plates, but finally you get a good hold on her. She's an evil witch, and you can't have her around, so you shove her in the oven and slam the door.

Well, that is the end of that. You straighten all the furniture back up and have a snack (jelly beans and cupcakes), then you decide to head back into the woods to keep looking for Granny.

You walk out the front door, but your stomach starts to hurt. Maybe you ate too much candy. You take another step. It hurts even worse. By the time you are ten feet away, you can't take it anymore. You run back to the cottage and eat a cookie. Instantly you feel better. So you have some more. And some more. And you

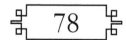

can't stop eating. At this rate, you are going to run out of candy.

You open the oven and see that Gretel has turned into a cake. You eat the cake and realize baking other people into snacks is the only way to get more food.

Even though your stomach is aching, you head out to the forest and wait for people to come by. When they do, you make up some story about an evil witch kidnapping your sister and needing their help. When they offer to help you, you bake them and eat them. If you could ever think of anything besides eating, you might try to find a way to break this curse, but until then, this seems like your only solution.

THE END

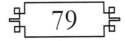

The men talk and talk and you think they will never shut up. Finally they go into a deeper room of the cave. Now is your chance to make your escape. You tiptoe out of the cave. But on the way, you can't resist taking just a few shiny gems and pieces of gold jewelry. Just enough to fit into your pockets.

When you turn, you trip on a treasure chest and it makes a really loud noise. Instantly the men rush out and see you. You say the magic words and run for the door. Of course they follow you. They want their treasure that you've just stolen.

"Come back, thief!" they call.

You don't listen. You keep running. You turn back to see how far behind you they are. They're only about

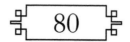

ten feet away. They are going to capture you and . . . you can't imagine what they will do. As you're imagining the worst, you turn back, just in time to run off a cliff. You should have been looking where you were going.

You fall forever. Surely you should have hit the ground and died by now. But you keep falling. You squeeze your eyes shut because you can't take it anymore, and when you finally open them, you realize that you aren't falling at all. You are in your bed at Granny's house.

Maybe it was all a dream. A very bad dream. Except when you reach into your pockets, you realize they are filled with jewels and gold treasure.

THE END

You decide to wait it out in the castle and hope your true love will come. The castle isn't all that bad. You do miss your granny, but you figure she's back in the real world wondering where you are.

Finally one day a girl shows up to the castle. You think she could be your true love, but all she does is run from you and throw things at you. This makes you really mad, and you yell and scream and act really undignified. She finally runs to her room, locks the door, and says that she will never be your true love and that she is never coming out again. You don't know why she just doesn't leave the castle. You're kind of sick of her, anyway.

You could tell her to leave. Or maybe you should try a little bit harder to be nice to her. After all, you haven't been the nicest monster.

*If you tell her to leave, turn to page 110.*

*If you try a little bit harder to make her like you, turn to page 102.*

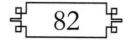

No way are you sticking around for one more song. That giant could capture you again if you aren't careful. You dash from the room and out of the castle.

The giant follows you, sniffing along your trail. You try to lose him by dashing in water and through mud, but he must have the best nose in Fairy Tale Land. Finally you reach the edge of his land.

You start down the beanstalk, and you climb as fast as you can. Pretty soon the beanstalk starts to shake. The giant is following you. He's shouting as he climbs, talking about all the ways he's going to make you into bread. You do not want to be made into bread.

When you finally reach the bottom, there's a woodcutter nearby. "Can I borrow your ax?" you ask him.

He gives you the ax and you start chopping down the beanstalk as fast as you can. It begins to wobble and shake, and then it collapses. Suddenly a giant shadow falls over you. You look up just in time to see the giant falling right for you. The last thought you have is that you really should have gotten out of the way. Then he lands on top of you.

# THE END

83

You stay just a little bit longer. Then a little longer. It's actually kind of fun being a bear. You look in the mirror one day and notice that you are actually growing thick brown fur all over your body. And your fingernails are turning into claws. You are turning into a bear! You have no idea how this is possible or if you can do anything about it.

But maybe that's not so bad. Your bear friends at preschool really like you and you like them. You get to play all day long. Life isn't so bad as a bear.

One day, after Mama and Papa Bear head out to collect some honey, someone knocks on the door. You open it and come face to face with another bear who looks exactly like you.

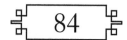

"I'm Baby Bear," you say. Maybe it's another bear from preschool that's new.

"No, I'm Baby Bear," the bear says, and he pushes his way inside. "No more taking over my life."

Then the real Baby Bear drags you outside and throws you over the side of a cliff. As you fall, you realize how much you will miss Mama and Papa Bear. But they won't miss you. They won't even know you're gone.

THE END

You take the job because there's a lot you don't know about this fairy tale world. If things out there are really trying to kill you, then you need to learn more about the world before you venture back out.

The shoemaker takes you into the back of the shop and shows you his shoemaking supplies. He teaches you how to use them, and you start making shoes. You make really nice shoes. They're shiny and soft and they fit customers perfectly. People come in and rave about them. The problem is that the shoemaker takes all the credit! They tell him that he's the best shoemaker in the world, and all he says is "Thank you." You're tempted to start making really bad shoes, except you really like making shoes, and you can't bring yourself to make

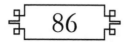

anything less than perfection. But still, this shoemaker is the worst. He sits around and does nothing while you do all the work.

One day, after you've made five amazing pairs of shoes, you ask him to pay you. So far, he hasn't paid a cent.

"Sorry, I can't afford to pay you," the shoemaker says.

Can't afford it! These shoes are selling for lots of money. You can't take this anymore. Either you need to leave this shoe shop or . . . you could do away with the shoemaker. You could run this place yourself.

---

*If you leave, turn to page 118.*

*If you do away with the shoemaker, turn to page 104.*

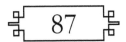

Mining for gold sounds like it could be profitable, but it's not your top priority. You need to find Granny and get out of here. "No thanks," you tell the dwarves.

Dwarves don't like to be told no. All their smiles turn to frowns and they start chasing you. Luckily your legs are a little longer than theirs, so you can run faster, but they have a ton of energy and never give up. You have to get away from them.

You climb up a hill and down to the other side, and there is a cave. You could hide inside. But maybe they'd expect you to hide inside. But maybe they'd expect you to expect them to know you were hiding inside. It's really confusing.

*If you hide in the cave, turn to page 106.*

*If you keep running, turn to page 111.*

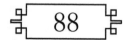

Y ou are not going to waste your only wish on revenge.

"I wish for a way out of Fairy Tale Land and back to my world," you tell the genie.

The genie bows. "As you wish." Then the genie turns into the old woman you ran into outside the castle, the one with the apple and the black fingernails.

She tells you that the only way she can grant your wish is if you find her a treasure. But she can't be serious? You had one wish. The wish should not have any conditions. This old lady/genie is not on the level.

You could play along with her game and try to find the treasure she wants, or you could run away from her.

---

*If you play along and tell her you will find her treasure, turn to page 119.*

*If you run away from her because she's bound to have more tricks, turn to page 138.*

Fine. You'll kiss someone even though it's the last thing you want to do. You close your eyes and kiss the first person you see. It's hardly even a real kiss, just a peck on the cheek. It's a girl and her eyes flutter open. She tells you that her name is Aurora and that she's been asleep for one hundred years. You've been tired, but you've never slept that long.

"You must have broken the curse," she says.

You don't know anything about a curse, but she tells you that an old witch put a curse on the castle and everyone inside. It sounds pretty bad. The only problem is that no one else wakes up.

"That means the curse hasn't been broken," Aurora says. And she starts to run for the front door of the

castle. "We have to get out now or the curse will capture us!"

You run after her because you don't want the curse to get you. You dash out the front door, and she falls behind. Then you stop.

Ahead of you in the path is Ella. She's holding a spear and pointing it directly at you. You turn to run back inside, but there is Aurora, holding a bow and arrow, also pointed at you.

"I got him," Aurora says.

"Great job!" Ella says.

Then they tie you to a tree outside and leave you there.

You struggle against the ropes, trying to get them loose, but Ella and Aurora are masters at tying knots. But you keep at it. Finally you feel a tiny amount of give. This will work. You'll be able to get yourself free. But before you can pull a hand out of the ropes, a giant wolf comes along. He takes one look at you, sniffs the air, and then eats you in a single bite.

THE END

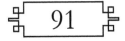

Ella had tried to lock you in an oven. That's already pretty bad. You decide you should believe the giant because you should never hide in an oven no matter what. Everyone knows that!

"I thought there was something not so nice about her," you say to the giant, and you walk away from the edge of the land. Maybe the two of you together can throw Ella over the side.

Just then, Ella walks up. But instead of walking to you, like you think she should, she walks right up to the giant and gives him a high five.

"Works every time!" Ella says.

What!?

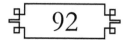

"If only you'd gotten him in the oven," the giant grumbles, then he reaches out a hand and grabs you around the waist.

This is the worst. You're sure he's going to throw you into the oven. You're wrong. Instead he lifts you to his giant mouth and tosses you inside, swallowing you whole. You try to think of a way to escape before he digests you, but you can't.

THE END

You go exactly where the bear family told you to go, and sure enough, there's a funny little house that looks like it's made of patchwork fabric. You knock on the door, and a short little man greets you. This must be the leprechaun!

You explain your problem, and he smiles.

"Of course I can help you," he says. "If you guess my name, I'll show you the way home. If you get it wrong, you lose."

You aren't sure what you lose, but you've heard this story before. There is no way you will get his name wrong.

"You're Rumpelstiltskin!" you say. Everyone has heard this story.

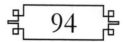

"Wrong!" he says. "My name is Rip Van Winkle. You humans always get that wrong."

Then he grabs a scroll from his shelf and unrolls it. Words curl off the pages and fly toward you. You try to duck out of their way, but they find you no matter how hard you try. Then you feel yourself changing.

When you look into the mirror, you see that you have turned into a hideous ogre! No one will ever talk to you again. You try to talk to people as you wander around Fairy Tale Land, but it's useless. Finally you decide to live under a bridge and eat anyone who tries to cross.

# THE END

Maybe you're really stupid, but you decide to help Gretel. She tells you exactly where to go and who to talk to in the town. Then she starts chewing on the door again. You grab a gumdrop from a nearby hedge and then set out toward the town.

It takes you two hours of solid walking to get to the town. You figure nobody wants to live too close to the cursed candy house. You ask around and you finally find a blue house where the old lady lives. You knock on the door, half expecting Gretel to be in there and this to all have been some sort of trick. But no. It really is an old lady. Actually it's the same old lady with the black fingernails who offered you the apple back by the castle.

"My friend Gretel needs help," you tell the old lady, and you explain the curse and the candy.

"Oh, I have just the thing," the old lady says. Or at least that's what you think she says. It's hard to understand her without any teeth.

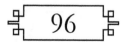
96

She hands you a jar with red potion and tells you to have Gretel drink it. Then she asks you to help her dust her shelves. You do, because she's a little old lady and you don't mind helping little old ladies. Then you leave.

When you get back to the house, Gretel has eaten the entire door and half the front wall of the house. You stay in the yard. "Drink this," you say, and you toss her the potion.

Gretel doesn't even question it. She gulps it down and throws the glass bottle onto the ground where it smashes. Then she runs away from the house and far into the woods.

"Thank you!" she says. "You saved me! And now, I'll do something for you. I actually am a powerful fairy, and I can send you back to your world."

It's the best news you've heard.

Gretel says a few words, spins you around a couple times, then taps you on the head. The next thing you know, the closet door is right in front of you. You rush to it, turn the knob, and walk out of the fairytale world forever . . . or so you hope.

THE END

You have to learn more about this world, and you have to look for your granny. You can always go back through the mirror once you've looked around. You venture out into the mirror world and look for Granny.

You ask a bunch of people if they've seen her, but the more you talk to them, the harder it is to understand what they're saying. In addition to their sentences being backwards, now it's like their words are backwards, too. You try to change the way you are talking, but that makes it worse. Finally you say something, and you don't even know what it means. But one of the people screams something and points at you, and everyone starts to chase you. They grab weapons like pitchforks and shovels, like they're trying to kill you.

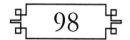

You run as fast as you can back to where you came through the mirror. You're going to reach it in time! Relief fills you. Finally you're right in front of it. But you press on it with your hand, and nothing happens. You can't get through.

From the other side you see the woman from the castle. She says, "Mirror, Mirror, on the wall, who is the Fairest of them all?"

"Who cares?!" you scream. "Just let me through."

Her eyes widen as she recognizes you. Then she smiles a really evil smile and picks up a heavy crystal vase. In a flash, she hits the mirror with it, shattering the glass. You knew she was evil!

The world around you starts to fade and turn black. Everything disappears. The tree. The people. The weapons. Everything except you. You're stuck there, in a world of nothing on the wrong side of the mirror forever.

THE END

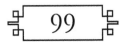

**D**eadly quests are just not your specialty, and you are not going to do it. You're pretty sure there's another way out of the cave because they don't seem to use the front rock door all that often.

"Can I go to the bathroom and think about it?" you ask.

They agree and point the way to the bathroom. They tell you to turn left, then left, then right.

You thank them then head deeper into the cave, in the direction they pointed. But you don't go to the bathroom. Instead you look for their secret exit. You try every side passageway you come to, but all you find are more piles of treasure. Then you really do have to use the bathroom, but you can't find it either.

You try to backtrack, but it only makes you get more lost. You sink down in a room filled with cushions and try to think. There is no way out of this cave. You are really lost. You can't even find your way back to the thieves to tell them that you'll do their quest.

Maybe one day, they'll find you. But until then, you are going to be wandering around lost forever.

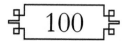

There is no way that nice little bear family is turning people into porridge. These villagers must be wrong.

"I think I saw the bears that way," you say, pointing in the opposite direction of where the bears are. Then you run back into the woods to warn the bears.

First you stop at the river, but there is no sign of Baby Bear. You hope angry villagers didn't get him already. Maybe he made it home.

When you get to the clearing with the cottage, you knock in the door. Papa Bear opens it. Mama Bear stands behind him with her hand on Baby Bear's head. He made it home! Now to keep them safe.

"You guys are in danger!" you tell them, and you explain about the angry villagers.

Papa Bear gives Mama Bear a small nod of his head, like they're agreeing on something. Then he grabs you and drags you into the cottage. You still can't accept what's happening even as they throw you into the giant porridge pot and put the lid on top.

# THE END

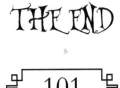

101

You are not going to give up on this girl so easily. You will be the nicest, most fun, most polite monster in the entire universe. You even adopt a dog who really likes to sleep in front of the fire. But the harder you try to be nice to the girl, the more horrible she is. Actually, she acts like a spoiled rotten monster. Finally you've had enough.

"Just leave me and my dog alone," you say, and you sit in your favorite chair in front of the fire and start reading a book.

Your dog can tell that you're upset. It comes over and licks you on your monstrous cheek. Immediately you turn back into a human. Dogs are true love.

The mean girl walks back in, sees you, and all of a sudden she starts acting really nice. But you are totally

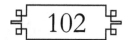

over her, and the harder she tries to be nice to you, the less you like her. Finally she stomps her foot and says she's leaving.

You open the door for her and close it the second she's through. Then you and your dog live in your castle happily. You always think about getting back to the real world, but it's not so bad here, especially with your dog. Maybe one day you'll try to leave, but that day is not today.

THE END

Enough of him getting all the credit. This shoemaker is going down. You visit the local spell maker, an old woman who lives in town. She completely understands your problem, and she gives you a potion.

When the shoemaker isn't looking, you mix it into his ale. He drinks the entire thing, burps, and then turns into a small green frog. Perfect!

The frog jumps, but you are fast, and you take a broom and sweep him out of the shop. Then you close the door and get to work making shoes.

You make even better shoes than before, and pretty soon you are known across the entire country as the best shoemaker ever. This is truly your calling in life. You never knew making shoes could be so rewarding.

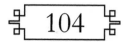

You wear the finest shoes of them all, made from the very best leather.

One day someone knocks on the door. Maybe it's a prince from a land far away who's come to get a pair of shoes. You open the door, and there is a giant frog.

Its tongue flicks out and wraps around you, and the frog pulls you into its mouth and eats you in a single swallow. The only thing left of you are the very fine shoes that came off your feet.

THE END

You run into the cave. Maybe, if it's really dark, the dwarves won't be able to see you. No sooner are you inside, the dwarves come to the entrance. But instead of following you inside, they slide a giant rock across the opening, sealing you in. Time for Plan B.

You can't go back the way you came, so your only choice is to go deeper into the cave and hope it leads somewhere. It looks like there might even be a light ahead.

You use your hands to feel your way forward, and the light keeps getting brighter. Pretty soon you enter a chamber that is lit up. At the center of the chamber is a lantern. It's what's giving off all the light. It also looks like it's made of shiny gold.

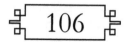

You run over to the lantern and pick it up. Is that writing on the side? You rub it off with your sleeve, and the next thing you know, a genie pops out of the lantern.

"You get one wish," the genie says. She's not all that friendly, and she almost looks annoyed that you've disturbed her. If anything, she should be thankful to not be locked in the tiny lantern any longer. But anyway, you get a wish.

You could wish for a way to get out of here and back home. But what about Granny? Or you could wish revenge on the stupid dwarves for locking you in here. That might be nice . . . Well, not so much for them.

---

*If you wish for a way home, turn to page 89.*

*If you wish for revenge on the dwarves, turn to page 126.*

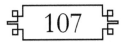

107

Kissing is gross. No way are you doing it. Instead you find an empty room and decide to stay here for a while, exploring the very quiet castle, eating the food, and playing all the fun castle games, like darts and ping pong. But there's no one to play with, and pretty soon you get a little bored. A lot bored. You need to get out of here.

You go back to the front door and try to open it, but it won't budge. A quick glance out the window tells you that huge vines with thorns have grown over the door, blocking your escape from this place. You need to find another way out. Maybe you can go out a window and climb down.

You head upstairs and look out a window. The vines don't reach this window. If you go out this way,

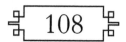

you will probably kill yourself trying to reach one of the vines.

Wait. Is that Ella out there in the meadow? It is. And she's watching you. You wave at her and call her name. She sees you and smiles. But it's not a really friendly smile. It's kind of mean, actually. Then she laughs and walks away.

Fine. You are going to have to kiss someone. But before you can leave the room, you get really tired. Maybe you can take just a little nap and work on your escape plan when you wake up.

You lie down in the nearest bed. You can't even keep your eyes open. You've never been this tired before. That's when you realize that you've fallen under the same curse as everyone else in the castle. Maybe someone will come to help. It's your last thought before you fall asleep.

THE END

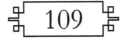

Y ou tell the girl to leave. She's a little reluctant to go, but whatever. You open the door, and out she goes.

She's not five steps away when a pack of wolves attacks her. You're out the door before you know it, and with your monster strength, you fight the wolves and tear them to shreds. Wow, it is actually pretty amazing being a monster after all. No way would you have been able to do that as a human.

The girl is really grateful. She throws her arms around you and hugs you, and she kisses you on the cheek. She's not your true love, so this doesn't change you back into a human. But she says, "I do have the power to change you back into a human . . . if you want."

Do you want to be a human again? Or do you want to be an amazing, strong, fierce monster? It's hard to decide.

*If you tell her you want to be human again, turn to page 130.*

*If you decide you want to stay a monster, turn to page 117.*

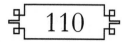

There is no way you are going into the cave. It's exactly what they would expect you to do. Instead you keep running, always staying just a little bit ahead of the seven dwarves.

Finally ahead, you get your first lucky break. There is a river, and leading across the river is a bridge. You dash out onto the bridge and then dare to turn back.

The dwarves have stopped a little bit back from the edge of the bridge and they watch you. But they aren't following. Maybe dwarves don't like water. Maybe they don't like bridges. Maybe they can't leave the mountains. Maybe . . .

You're thinking up all the possible maybes when from under the bridge a giant ogre appears. It opens its gaping mouth and lunges right for you.

Your last thought is 'Maybe there's an ogre living under the bridge.' Then the ogre eats you.

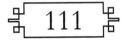

111

You jump back through the mirror as quickly as you possibly can. There is no need to spend any longer than normal in the mirror world. But when you get back to the castle, the woman is waiting for you.

"You were trying to steal my mirror!" she screams, and before you can protest, she has you thrown into the dungeon. You hate being accused of something you didn't do, but none of the guards will listen to you as you try to convince them. They toss you into a cell and they lock the door behind you.

Even here in the dungeon the food is really good. The guards bring you three meals a day and dessert. When you ask for second helpings, they go back to the buffet to get you more. It's not all that bad.

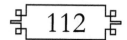

One day another prisoner is brought into the dungeon. The guards throw her into the cell next to you.

"My name is Ella," she tells you, and you guys quickly become friends. She's wearing a really glittery dress and glass shoes which look horribly uncomfortable.

Ella doesn't seem as excited about the food as you are, and one day she suggests you guys come up with a plan to escape. Escape would be nice. You could look for Granny and find a way back to your own world. But the food is pretty good here in the dungeon. And they may let you out if you have good behavior.

---

***If you agree to an escape plan, turn to page 134.***

***If you tell Ella no thanks and stay in the dungeon, turn to page 120.***

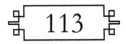

The thieves smile and slap you on the back and tell you that you are brave. You don't feel very brave. But maybe this quest will make you braver.

They drag out a small rolled-up carpet and hand it to you.

"This is a magic flying carpet," one of them says. "Fly on it to the castle and steal some figs from the fig tree at the very center of the castle garden."

That doesn't sound so bad. It actually sounds kind of tasty. They open the door of the cave, and you unroll the carpet, place it on the ground, and then sit on it.

It immediately starts lifting off the ground, and the next thing you know, you are flying!

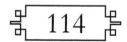
114

You fly through the air, all across the land of fairy tales. You see everything and everyone, and you wave when you go by. You almost feel like a famous rock star.

Soon you see the castle, but you decide to wait until night. When night finally comes, you fly over the walls of the castle and into the garden. There, in the center, is the nicest fig tree ever with figs as big as your fists. You eat at least five. Maybe six. Then you fill the basket that the thieves gave you with figs.

As you're walking back to your carpet, you spot something coming right for you. It's a tiger!

---

***If you try to make a run for it to the carpet, turn to page 124.***

***If you try to fight off the tiger, turn to page 141.***

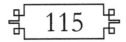

You can't believe a giant! Sure, Ella tried to get you inside an oven, but she was only trying to protect you. You rush to the edge of the giant's land. The giant follows, just like you planned. At the very last second you grab hold of the giant vine so you don't fall.

The giant is not expecting this. He's moving fast, and he can't stop. You watch as he tumbles off the edge and falls and falls and falls. You can't see him after he passes into the clouds. But the ground shakes when he hits far below.

"We did it!" Ella says running up and hugging you. "I've been his prisoner for as long as I can remember."

You're just happy you were able to help.

"Do you know a way I can get back to my world?" you ask Ella.

She shakes her head. "No. But while you look, we could rule here in the giant's land as king and queen. The people would be really happy to have nice rulers."

It doesn't sound like a bad plan, so that is exactly what you do.

THE END

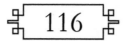

You think long and hard about it, but you finally decide.

"I want to stay a monster," you tell her. Being a monster is awesome. You could make it your mission to rid the surrounding lands of any threats like the wolves. It's not the life you imagined, but it is a good life.

"I don't blame you," she says. "I always wanted to be a monster, too."

She tells you that she has to get back to her family, but you're both kind of sad when she leaves.

A week goes by and you hear a knock on the door. When you open it, there she is with a box in her hands.

"I thought I could come visit once a week to play board games," she says.

That's the best thing you've ever heard.

You make hot chocolate with extra whipped cream for both of you, and you play the game. Every week it's a different game, and every week you guys get along a little bit better. Maybe she's not your true love, but she is now your best friend.

THE END

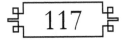

Just because the shoemaker is a jerk doesn't mean you should do away with him. You pack your bags and sneak out early one morning before he is awake. You know he'd never let you leave on your own.

You travel across the land until you find another shop. There you use the one pair of shoes you brought with you to finance opening a shoe shop. You make amazing shoes and people come from far around to buy them. You hire an apprentice and teach her how to make the shoes. Then you leave the shop to her and travel to another town to do the same. You do this over and over, and pretty soon everyone knows your shoes.

Every so often you think about trying to find a way back to the real world, but you really love the shoe empire you've created. You decide to stay and re-brand your shoe stores under the name Grannydidas, in honor of your granny. You live happily there the rest of your days.

# THE END

Y ou don't want to go any deeper in the cave, but you also need to get out of here. You agree to the old woman's deal. You set out, going deeper and deeper. You find all sorts of cool things, like diamonds and rubies and redstone, but you don't find the treasure she's talking about. You almost don't think it exists.

One day, you're chipping away at some rocks when you hit a hollow spot. Suddenly the rocks fall away, and there it is. This is the treasure the old lady was talking about. It's a golden set of armor along with golden weapons. Whoever wears this armor will never be defeated.

You grab it quickly and start back for the old woman. But wait. Why should she get this treasure? You're the one who found it. You could keep it and never return to her.

---

*If you bring the treasure back to the old woman, turn to page 127.*

*If you keep the treasure for yourself, turn to page 131.*

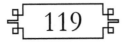

Ella seems pretty nice, but this fairy tale world is full of creatures that are not what they seem to be. Otherwise you would never be here in this dungeon in the first place.

"I'm going to stay here," you tell Ella.

A tear slips down her face. "I'll miss you," she says.

Whatever. You fall asleep. When you wake up, she's gone. She really did escape, all on her own.

A day goes by. You eat some food. You think a lot . . . about Ella. And you realize that even though you didn't know her very well, you really miss her. You need to get out of here and find her.

You come up with your own plan. When the guard brings you food, you fake being sick. He completely falls for it and unlocks the door. You hit him upside the

head and run from the cell, never looking back. Okay, you take one last look at the buffet table in the dining hall. Then you leave the castle.

Once you're in the woods where the guards can't see you, you notice a trail of glitter on the ground. It has to be from Ella's dress. She's left you a trail. You should follow it and find her. But you also need to look for your Granny. And get home.

---

*If you follow Ella's trail, turn to page 136.*

*If you try to find a way home, turn to page 128.*

You tell the angry mob where you saw the bears. The bears had seemed nice, but making humans into porridge is just wrong. After the angry mob runs off, you head to the village.

Pretty much every single person who lives here is part of the angry mob, so nobody is around. You go from house to house, trying to find someone who will tell you how to get out of this place. You really miss your granny, and you want to get home. It makes you kind of sad when you think about it.

Finally you knock on a door. From inside someone calls, "Come in."

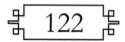

It sounds like a little old lady! Maybe it's Granny.

You open the door and go inside. The lights are really low, but it's bright enough to see that there is a little old lady lying in bed.

"Granny?" you say.

"Come closer," the old lady says.

She had on Granny's hat and jacket. It must be her. You rush over to the bed because you are so happy you found her. But Granny has a really long nose. And big teeth. And huge eyes. And when Granny opens her mouth to eat you, you realize that it's not Granny at all. It is a wolf, and you are its next meal.

THE END

You can't fight a tiger! That would be crazy. You make a run for the carpet, but before you can reach it, the tiger jumps over your head and lands in front of the carpet. Then it tears the carpet to shreds! That was your only way out of here. You run from the tiger, looking for somewhere to go, but every turn you take, the tiger is there. It's almost like it's guarding you.

You dash up some stairs, but when you are halfway up, a trapdoor opens and you fall inside.

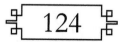
124

"We got another one," someone says, and they dress you in a black and white outfit that matches what a bunch of other people are wearing.

You try to explain your situation, but they don't care. "Save it for someone who cares," the person says. And then they tell you that you are the newest servant and that your job is now to clean the castle.

You clean and look for a way to escape. Every time you think you see a way out of here, the tiger appears. It's unbelievable. Night. Day. It's always there. You keep trying though, but you never escape. Finally you give up and resign yourself to cleaning the castle forever. They tell you that if you work hard enough, you may be promoted to cook. The king's favorite recipe is fig pie.

THE END

Those dwarves need to pay for what they did. Nobody locks you in a cave and gets away with it.

"I wish for revenge against the dwarves," you tell the genie.

The genie starts laughing. You aren't sure what's so funny.

The genie says, "The best way for you to get revenge on those dwarves is for you to take my place as the genie."

Before you can argue that this isn't the best way, the genie unclasps the gold bracelets from her wrists and slaps them on your wrists. Then the top of the lantern opens, and the next thing you know you are being sucked inside. You are now the genie.

You sit there, in the lantern, and you plot your revenge. When those dwarves find you—oh, and they will find you—you will make sure that whatever they wish for goes horribly wrong.

# THE END

A promise is a promise, and you did promise her that you would bring back the treasure to her. You start back.

It takes you a while to find the right place, but you finally reach the room with the genie lantern.

"Here is your treasure," you say, and you give her the armor and weapons. You only hope she uses them for good.

She puts them on and turns beautiful. She almost glows. Then she tells you that she is a good witch and that with this armor, her full power has been restored. Then she waves her wand a few times and says some funny riddle about a cow jumping over the moon. With every word she says, you get sleepier.

Finally you fall to the ground, fast asleep. When you wake up, you are in the rocking chair, back at your granny's house. Granny is just covering you up with a blanket and putting a pillow under your head.

"Sweet dreams," Granny says.

Was the entire thing a dream?

THE END

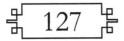

Sure, Ella was nice, but you only knew her for less than a day. You need to find your granny and get out of Fairy Tale Land!

You find a town and ask around about your granny. Someone says that she did come through here, but that she found a way back to her world. This is great news. The town people tell you that what you need to do is go find an old lady who lives in a shoe. She can help you get back to your world.

You have no idea why anyone would live in a shoe, but who are you to judge? You set out on the path the townspeople tell you, and pretty soon, down in a valley, you see a giant shoe. You run down the hill toward it. Sure enough, inside is a woman about your mom's age who lives there. There are also at least twenty kids

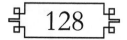

running around who live there. No wonder it's such a big shoe, with that many people living in it.

The shoe kind of smells like dirty feet, but you aren't going to be here long.

"Can you help me get home?" you ask the lady.

"Sure," she says. "But first can you stay here for a few minutes while I run to the grocery store?"

You've never babysat before, but it can't be that hard. You agree.

The lady goes out, up the hill, toward town. Night comes. She's still not back. She doesn't return the next day. Or the next. You finally accept the fact that she's never coming back. What are you supposed to do now? You can't leave these kids. They need you. And love you. And so you stay there raising them forever.

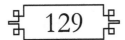

S ure, being a monster is pretty cool, but you really liked being a human.

"Please turn me back into a human," you say.

The girl giggles. "I was just kidding!" she says, like it's a really funny joke.

You don't find it funny at all.

The girl runs off, back outside since it's now free of the wolves. You almost run after her because you are really mad. You want to tear something else apart. But instead you go inside the castle and slam the door because you remember something your granny said about not doing anything when you're mad because you'll regret it.

Maybe you'll go after the girl when you aren't so mad. Except you stay mad the rest of that day. And the next day. The next month. Then year. You don't think you're ever going to get over being mad, and that's just fine with you. After all, angry monsters are even scarier than nice monsters.

## THE END

130

After all your hard work finding this treasure, there is no way you are bringing it back to the old woman. You'll find your own way out of here.

You tie it into a pack and start walking, looking for a way out. The cave is a huge maze, and you always seem to take the wrong turn. You backtrack, but nothing looks the same. If you don't do something, you are going to be stuck in this cave forever.

Finally you have an idea. You unpack the armor and weapons and put them on. Maybe they have some kind of magical powers.

They seem to get heavier when you put them on. They didn't feel this heavy when you were carrying them. You try to take a step but can't lift your foot. When you look down, you see why. You are now sunken into the ground to your knees. As you watch, you sink to your waist. Then your stomach. The more you struggle, the faster you sink. Pretty soon the sand is over your head.

At least you will spend the last minutes of your life with your treasure. But you don't think it was worth it.

# THE END

You don't have time to help Gretel. You also don't believe her. This has to all be a trick so she can get you back inside the cottage and make you into a soufflé. You run away from the cottage, and you never look back.

It starts to get dark pretty soon, and since you're in the woods, it feels even darker. You need to find somewhere to sleep for the night. You look for a few trees that are close together, and you sink down against one of them and fall asleep.

You wake up in the middle of the night to a bunch of animals howling. It sounds like all sorts of different noises. And they're getting closer to you. You can't stay here. You stand up and run away from your hiding spot. Almost like they can smell you, the animals start howling louder. And getting even close. And you're sure in that instant that you are being hunted . . . by them!

This is the worst. You run through the trees, but now they're coming at you from all sides, and pretty soon, you are surrounded.

The animals have torches and they come into focus. They're like monsters that have been created from animal parts, and in seconds they are on you, tying you up.

"Let's take it back to the castle and eat it there," one of them that looks like a tiger says.

Eat you! You try to scream, but they stuff an apple in your mouth and you can't talk.

"And the head can be a trophy," another of the animals says. It looks like a pig.

You fight against them, but you don't have a chance. When they reach the castle and open the door, you finally pass out from fear. It's the last thing you remember.

THE END

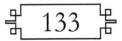

You can't stay locked up for the rest of your life just because the food is good. You tell Ella that you'd be happy to be part of an escape plan.

Ella is really smart, and she manages to get the keys from the guards. Once the guards are gone, she unlocks your cells, and you guys run out of the dungeon and escape the castle. You grab a few pastries for the road.

The two of you set off across the land of fairy tales because Ella tells you that she lives in a town far from the castle. You travel for days and nights, and after a month, you finally see two travelers on the road. One of them is riding a huge horse, and he stops alongside you guys.

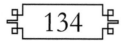

"Ella!" he says. "My love! I have been looking everywhere for you."

His love? What is all that about?

"Oh, Prince Charming!" Ella says. And then she tells you that she is engaged to the guy.

The guy frowns at you and then whispers something to his traveling companion. The traveling companion, you realize, is a wizard. He pulls out a wand, and with a quick wave of his hand, he turns you into a frog. Then Prince Charming picks you up and throws you into a nearby pond.

You watch as they ride away.

You sit on a lily pad and plot your revenge. You will set off toward the town and find someone to turn you back into a person. But you keep getting distracted by eating flies. They taste so good. Just one more and then you'll start out on your journey for revenge. Just one more.

THE END

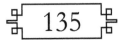

You follow Ella's trail because you can't get her out of your head. The trail is pretty easy to follow because so much glitter seems to fall off her dress. You finally reach a town, and they tell you that yes, she was here, but that she left. This happens again, and again. She always stays one step ahead of you.

You double your pace because each day you realize you are more and more in love with her. You have to find her even if it is all you ever do.

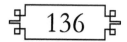

One day you come to a castle. There on the steps of the castle is a single glass shoe. You have no idea why someone would wear shoes made of glass, but Ella had walked okay in them. You pick up the shoe. This is it. She must be inside the castle!

"There is the thief!" someone shouts, and before you know what's happening, guards are running for you.

You take off, running away from them. You can't let them capture you because if they do, you'll never be with Ella. They follow you for a while but finally give up. You're left with the glass shoe and your dreams of being with Ella forever. You will never give up on your dreams. Never.

THE END

This old lady/genie cannot be trusted.

"No way am I playing your games!" you yell at her, and then you run, deeper into the cave.

You round a corner, and there's an apple on the ground. When you look up, the old lady is directly in front of you. It's impossible, and yet it happened.

You turn and run back the other way. The same thing happens. Then again. She's still playing more games with you.

"Fine, I'll get your treasure," you say the next time she cuts you off.

She smiles, showing her empty gums. "Don't you see? You are the treasure," she says.

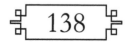

138

Then she snaps her fingers and a giant cage falls from the ceiling and captures you. You are trapped inside. You touch the bars, but they must have electricity running through them because they shock you.

"Now sing for me," she says.

You have the worst singing voice in the history of the world, but you sing. And she really likes it. You try to sing really badly so maybe she'll let you go, but the worse you sing, the more she likes it. Finally you give up and sink to the ground, hoping she'll give up on you.

"I'll make you one final deal," she says. "If you can sing me the best song ever, I'll let you go."

You don't believe her, but you try, really hard. And you keep trying, day after day. Your song is never good enough, and you stay trapped there forever.

# THE END

You step forward and begin talking to the evil sea witch. She tries to grab you, but before she can, you challenge her to a riddle competition. If you win, you get the necklace. If she wins, she gets to keep you in a cage. You really hope you win.

You take your time coming up with and answering riddles. You can't afford to make a mistake. But the sea witch is horrible at riddles, and after three, you stump her and she loses. She's good to her word though, and she gives you the necklace.

You swim out of her lair and back to the hiding mermaid. When you give her the necklace, she puts it on, and instantly she can speak again.

"You must come back to my people," she says, and she brings you in front of her dad, who happens to be the sea king (a nice sea king). He has a huge celebration then offers to change you into a merperson . . . if you want. It seems like they lead a pretty nice life, and the water is nowhere near as cold as you thought it would be, so you agree. You are now one of them. You live the rest of your days there under the water, staying far away from the evil sea witch.

## THE END

140

You jump forward and start fighting the tiger. But the tiger thinks you are playing with it! It tosses you a ball, and you roll it back. Over and over the tiger does this. Then it lets you scratch it behind the ears. Finally you realize you have to get back to the thieves. You eat a few more figs, then step back onto the magic carpet.

"Are you coming?" you ask the tiger.

It jumps on and sits next to you.

The carpet flies you back to the cave of the forty thieves, and when you arrive with the tiger, they are really impressed. So impressed, in fact, that they declare you their leader.

As you live and steal stuff with them, you realize that they aren't actually bad guys at all. Sure, they steal stuff, but it's from really rich people who don't appreciate it. And they help poor people and people who are in trouble all the time. And now, with your tiger, you and the forty thieves vow to rid Fairy Tale Land of evil once and for all. It is a worthy life.

# THE END

141

## A NOTE FROM CONNOR

### To all the Fairy Tale Lovers out there:

Thank you so much for taking the time to read *Pick Your Own Quest: Trapped in a Fairy Tale*! It's readers like you who will keep imagination alive!

If you did enjoy reading *Pick Your Own Quest: Trapped in a Fairy Tale*, I would love if you would take a few moments to review the book on Amazon. Reviews are so important these days, and even a one sentence review can make a huge difference in other readers discovering the series.

Now go dream up some new worlds (or read another book)!

—CONNOR HOOVER

LIKE VIDEO GAMES?
THINK MAGIC AND MONSTERS
ARE COOL?

LOOK FOR

A SERIES BY
CONNOR HOOVER!

LIKE ADVENTURE STORIES?
THINK ALIENS ARE COOL?

LOOK FOR

A SERIES BY
CONNOR HOOVER!

# LOOK FOR

Ancient Egypt is in serious trouble…

Crazy things are happening in Egypt! The gods are angry. The Nile River is drying up. Smoke appears on the horizon. Crocodiles attack! It's up to you to save the world. Make the right choice and you get to rule Egypt for the rest of your life. Make the wrong choice and it will be your last.

Remember, you can't turn back. Sorry! Once you make a choice, it can't be changed.

**CHOOSE WISELY :)**

## ABOUT THE AUTHOR

Connor Hoover thought living in Fairy Tale Land would be kind of fun except for all the wolves, bears, and evil stepmothers. Instead Connor lives in Austin, Texas with a magic mirror and dreams up new twists on old stories.

To contact Connor:

connor@connorhoover.com
www.connorhoover.com